Ling & Ting

Share a Birthday

by Grace Lin

Ⓛ Ⓑ
LITTLE, BROWN AND COMPANY
New York · Boston

To Hazel Maisy

and all her future happy birthdays

Little, Brown and Company

Hachette Book Group
1290 Avenue of the Americas, New York, NY 10104
Visit our website at lb-kids.com

Little, Brown and Company is a division of Hachette Book Group, Inc.
The Little, Brown name and logo are trademarks of Hachette Book Group, Inc.

The publisher is not responsible for websites (or their content) that are not owned by the publisher.

First Paperback Edition: September 2014
First published in hardcover in September 2013 by Little, Brown and Company

Lin, Grace.
Ling & Ting share a birthday / by Grace Lin.—1st ed.
p. cm.
Summary: "Identical twins Ling and Ting celebrate their birthday by sharing gifts and making wishes." —Provided by publisher.
ISBN 978-0-316-18405-2 (hc)—ISBN 978-0-316-18404-5 (pb)
[1. Twins—Fiction. 2. Sisters—Fiction. 3. Birthdays—Fiction. 4. Chinese Americans—Fiction.] I. Title. II. Title: Ling and Ting share a birthday.
PZ7.L644Lip 2013
[E]—dc23
2012040965

10 9 8 7 6

APS

Printed in China

The illustrations for this book were done in Turner Design Gouache on Arches hot-pressed watercolor paper. The text was set in StoneInfITC Medium, the display type was hand-lettered by the author.

Passport to Reading titles are leveled by independent reviewers applying the standards developed by Irene Fountas and Gay Su Pinnell in *Matching Books to Readers: Using Leveled Books in Guided Reading*, Heinemann, 1999.

6 Stories

We are twins, but we are not exactly the same!

Can you see how?

Story 1

Birthday
Shoes

Ling and Ting are twins. They share many things. They share the same dark eyes. They share the same blue dresses. They also share the same birthday!

"Look, Ling!" Ting says. "We have a gift!
It is a birthday gift!"

"Let us open it," Ling says. "Let us see
what it is."

Ling and Ting open the gift. Inside are two pairs of shoes. One pair of shoes is green. The other pair of shoes is red.

"New shoes!" Ting says. "Birthday shoes!"

"Yes," Ling says. "There is one pair of birthday shoes for me. There is one pair of birthday shoes for you. It is because we share a birthday."

"I will take the red birthday shoes,"
says Ting.

"I will take the green birthday shoes,"
says Ling.

Ling and Ting put on their shoes. Ling looks at Ting. Ting looks at Ling. They share the same eye color. They share the same dress color. They do not share the same shoe color.

"Our birthday shoes are not the same," Ling says.

"No," Ting says.

"But we share the same birthday," Ling says. "Our shoes should be the same, too."

"I know!" Ting says. "We will share the birthday shoes!"

Ling and Ting are twins. They share
many things. They share a birthday.
They share birthday shoes, too.

Story 2

Birthday Shopping

Ling and Ting are going shopping. Ling wants to buy a birthday gift for Ting. Ting wants to buy a birthday gift for Ling. But they want the gifts to be secret.

"Ting," Ling says, "I want to go to this store alone."

"I want to go to a store alone, too," says Ting. "You can go to this store. I will go to another store."

Ling goes into a bookstore. She looks at all the books. She sees a book that she wants to read.

"I will buy this book for Ting," Ling says. "Maybe she will share it with me."

Ting goes into a toy store. She looks at all the toys. She sees a toy that she wants to play with.

"I will buy this toy for Ling," Ting says. "Maybe she will share it with me."

Ling and Ting meet after shopping.

"What did you buy?" Ling asks Ting.

"It is a secret," says Ting. "What did you buy?"

"It is a secret, too," Ling says.

Ling and Ting look at each other. They walk home. They do not share their secrets. But they do share the same secret smiles.

Story 3

Ling and Ting are ready to bake.

"We should have two birthday cakes," Ting says. "There should be one cake for you. There should be one cake for me. It is a birthday for both of us."

"Yes," Ling says. "I will bake my cake. You will bake your cake."

Ling reads the cookbook very carefully.
She mixes butter, sugar, eggs, and flour.

Ting does not read the cookbook carefully.
She mixes butter, sugar, and eggs.

Ling and Ting put their cakes in the oven.
They watch them bake. Ling's cake bakes
golden. Ting's cake does not.

"My cake did not bake!" Ting says.
"My cake is not good."

Ting eats a small bite of her cake. Yuck! It does not taste like cake.

"My cake is bad!" Ting says. "Now I have no birthday cake!"

Ting is very sad. She tries not to cry.

"Do not worry," Ling says. "We will share my cake. I will cut it into two cakes. Then we will each have a cake."

Ling cuts her cake into two. Now Ling has a cake and Ting has a cake.

"Ling," Ting says, "I am glad I share a
birthday with you."

Story 4

Birthday Wishes

"**W**e forgot the most important thing!"

"What?" Ling says.

"We forgot to make a wish!" Ting says.
"We should put candles on the cake.
Then we should sing 'Happy Birthday.'
Then we should try to blow out all the
candles. If you blow out all your candles,
your wish comes true!"

"Yes!" Ting says. "We must make a wish!"

Ling puts candles on her cake. Ting puts candles on her cake.

Ling lights her candles. Ting sings "Happy Birthday" to Ling. Ling takes a breath. Ling blows.

One candle does not go out.

"One of my candles did not go out,"
Ling says. "I do not get a wish."

Ling is very sad. She tries not to cry.

"Do not worry," Ting says. "We will share my wish. I will wish that we both have wishes. Then we will each have a wish."

Ling sings "Happy Birthday" to Ting.
Ting takes a big breath. Ting blows.
All the candles go out.

Ting makes her wish. Now Ting has a wish and Ling has a wish.

"Ting," Ling says, "I am glad I share a birthday with you."

Story 5

Birthday Gifts

Now Ling gives Ting her gift. Ting gives Ling her gift.

"Happy birthday!" they say together. They open the gifts.

"I hope you like the book," Ling says. "Maybe you will share it with me."

"I hope you like the toy," Ting says.
"Maybe you will share it with me."

Ling and Ting like their gifts. But they like the other's gift a little bit more.

"I can share the book with you now,"
Ting says. "I will read it later."

"I can share the toy with you now,"
Ling says. "I will play with it later."

Ling reads the book and Ting plays with the toy.

"Thank you for the birthday gift," Ling says. "I like it very much."

"Thank you for the birthday gift," Ting says. "I like it very much, too."

"**W**hat is the book about?" Ting asks Ling.

"It is about twins," Ling says. "Their names are Ming and Sing. It is their birthday."

"Ming and Sing?" Ting asks. "I like those names. Let us pretend you are Ming and I am Sing. Tell me what they do."

"First," Ling says, "they wear their birthday mittens. Ming wears blue mittens and Sing wears green mittens."

"They do not share their birthday mittens?" Ting asks.

"No," Ling says. "Then, Ming and Sing make birthday cookies. Ming's cookies taste good. Sing's cookies taste bad."

"Ming does not share her birthday cookies?" Ting asks. "Maybe I do not want to pretend I am Sing."

"Then, Ming and Sing open their presents," Ling says. "Ming gets socks. Sing gets underwear."

"Underwear!" Ting says. "I do not want underwear! I changed my mind. I do not want to be Sing."

"Oh, I forgot!" Ling says. "Ming and Sing also make birthday wishes. What do you wish, Sing?"

"I wish that we are not Ming and Sing," Ting says. "I wish that we are Ling and Ting and we share a good birthday!"

"Ting! Guess what?" Ling says. "Your wish came true!"

"Yes," Ting says. "I guess it did."

★ ARTIST'S NOTE ★

The illustrations in this book were painted using Turner Design Gouache on Arches hot-pressed watercolor paper. The images and clothing were inspired by 1950s children's textbook illustrations, though interpreted with my own modern take. —*Grace Lin*

★ ABOUT THIS BOOK ★

This book was edited by Alvina Ling and designed by Saho Fujii under the art direction of Patti Ann Harris. The production was supervised by Jonathan Lopes, and the production editor was Christine Ma. This book was printed on 128-gsm Gold Sun matte paper. The text was set in StoneInfITC Medium, and the display type was hand-lettered by the author.

Yes! You are right! Our hair and shoes are different.

You can find out why our hair is different in our other book, "Ling & Ting: Not Exactly the Same!"